HUSTLA'S HOLIDAY

Slay & Kamille

Tip Montana

HUSTLA'S HOLIDAY
SLAY & KAMILLE

A TIP MONTANA STORY

Kamille

"I can't believe you're leaving me for the holidays," my best friend Yandy pouted as she helped me pack a few last-minute items.

"We'll only be gone a week, Yandy." I laughed as I zipped up my suitcase.

It was six days 'til Christmas, and I couldn't be happier. Christmas has always been my favorite time of the year. I loved to see all the beautiful decorations, Christmas trees, and of course the Christmas music. It's the time of year where families got together to exchange gifts and eat great food.

As a child, I would watch Christmas movies with my little brother and drink hot chocolate. I pictured waking up on Christmas morning, and the ground would be covered in snow. I would open my gifts and then run outside to build snowmen, make snow angels, and have snowball fights with the neighborhood kids. However, growing up in Florida, it was always hot this time of the year. Christmas morning here consisted of ninety-degree weather and kids outside riding their new bikes or scooters. There were no

Christmas carolers and definitely no snow.

Since I've become an adult, I always made it a point to go all out for Christmas, but this year it was going to be a little different. All I ever wanted was a white Christmas, so this year my wonderful husband planned an extended weekend getaway for the two of us in Breckinridge, Colorado. He rented us a cabin in the mountains and said he had all types of things planned. When he first told me, I cried tears of joy. I was finally going to get the white Christmas that I've always dreamed about. I couldn't wait to get there to play in the snow.

"A four days is a long time, Kami," Yandy continued to whine.

"I'll be back before you can miss me," I assured Yandy as I zipped up my last bag.

Looking around the room, I did a mental checklist to ensure I had everything I needed for the next week: *soap, lotion, deodorant, toothbrush.* Lord knows I would hate to forget something important and have to hunt down the nearest Walmart. I know Slay was probably cursing me out for packing all this stuff, but a girl could never have too many things.

"Why can't I come with y'all?" Yandy quizzed as we began to drag the luggage downstairs.

"Because bitch, this is a romantic getaway for my husband and me. I don't need yo' lonely ass following me."

"Bitch!" she yelled, slightly nudging me.

"I'm just playing." I laughed as I hug her.

Yandy and I have been best friends for years. We've been through the storm and the rain together, and there was nothing we wouldn't do for each other. She was like the sister I never had, and I would go to war with anybody about her.

"Anyway," she exclaimed, "make sure you take lots of pictures, and don't forget to call me when y'all land."

"I will, and I won't."

"And don't worry about the business. I have everything covered."

About a year after Slay and I got married, I started my interior decorating company named Millie's Designs. I've always had a passion for decorating but just never had the time to do it. When I told Slay how I wanted to open my own design studio, and he was all for it. I've been in business for two years now, and we were doing quite well. I hired Yandy as my assistant and taught her everything I knew. I wouldn't trust anyone else to run my business while I was gone.

"Yandy, thank you again for taking over for me."

"Girl, don't mention it," she commented with the wave of her hand. "Just make sure I get a nice Christmas bonus."

"Is this the last bag?" my brother-in-law, Terell, asked, coming into the house.

"Yes, this is the last one," I answered.

"What's up, Yandy? You looking good." He smirked, looking her up and down.

"Whatever nigga." Yandy replied, rolling her eyes at him.

Yandy and Terell used to have a thing a few years ago, but it didn't work out. Terell liked to have multiple females, and my girl wasn't going for that shit. Their relationship was one of the most toxic I'd ever seen.

"Oh, before I forget," I mentioned turning back toward Yandy. "My phone will be on DND, so here is the number to the resort in case of an emergency. And by emergency, I mean somebody better be dead or dying," I clarified, handing Yandy a piece of paper with the resort information on it. I didn't want any distractions while we were in Colorado.

"Okay, cool."

Glancing around the living room for the last time, I made

sure everything was in place before heading to the kitchen to do the same. Slay always said I did too much whenever we got ready to go on a trip, but I just wanted to make sure everything was turned off and secure. I'd hate to return home, and the place be burned to the ground.

"Kamille, you and your OCD are driving me crazy." Yandy laughed as I checked the knobs on the stove.

"I can't help it, Yandy." I shrugged.

"I tell you what. Let's take a few shots before you leave," Yandy suggested, pulling out a bottle of Tequila.

"Girl, you read my mind." I smiled as I grabbed two shot glasses from the bar.

She poured us both a shot, and we raised our glasses in the air.

"To my best friend. Have a safe trip, enjoy yourself, have plenty of nasty ass sex, and don't forget to bring me something back."

We both laughed as we threw our shots back. Now I was ready to have some fun.

"Bro, you sure you don't need me to go up there with you?" my brother Terell, but we call him Dirty, asked as he helped me load the truck with our luggage. You would've thought we were going to be gone for a month instead of a week with as much shit as Kamille packed.

"Naw, everything should be good," I assured him as I put the last bag in the trunk. Closing it, I grabbed the blunt from behind my ear and lit it. I needed to get faded before we headed to the airport.

"How much do you really know about this nigga, though? I mean shit, for all you know, this could be some type of set up," Dirty argued while taking the blunt from me.

"I doubt it's a setup. I mean, if it were, why would the nigga fly us all the way to Colorado just to kill me?"

"Stranger things have happened, nigga. You strapped, right?"

"Nigga, now you know me better than that. No matter

where I'm at, I'm always strapped," I said as I showed him just how heavily armed I really was.

My carry-on bag had a secret compartment where I had a few of my guns stashed, so I wasn't worried about security finding anything. I've been in the game a long time, and the last thing I would ever let a nigga do was catch me slipping.

My brother and I were both arms dealers. We could get you any kind of gun and ammunition you needed. Shit, we could even get you land mines and grenades if your money were right. We've been in the game for over ten years, and it's been incredibly good to us.

When I first got the invite from Darnael Bellevue to meet up, I was a little skeptical. I mean, I didn't know dude but being in this type of business, you hear about certain people. From what I gather, he was an upstanding type of guy and about business. I wasn't sure why he wanted to meet me, but I was always down to make some connections and more money. I figured I'd go see what he was talking about, and if it sounded legit, we could do business.

Darnael and his wife Blair had arranged for us to fly out to Breckinridge, Colorado, on a private jet. This was perfect because I was looking to take Kamille somewhere for the holidays, anyway. She always said she wanted to see snow, and the fact that it was snowing this time of year was perfect. They set us up at Grand Colorado on Peak 8 Resort for an extended weekend. From the pictures Kami showed me, the resort was nice, so I was looking forward to it.

"Just make sure if some shit seems out of place, you follow yo' gut," Dirty advised.

"Nigga," I chuckled, "I'm the one who taught you the game. I got this."

We continued smoking and talking until Kamille and Yandy come outside.

"You ready to go, bae?" Kamille asked, hugging my waist.

"Yeah, I'm ready," I replied as I kissed her lips. I could tell her and Yandy had been drinking because I could taste it on her lips.

"Alright, girl, I'mma miss you!" Yandy cried as she and Kamille hugged each other.

"Y'all be safe. Call me as soon as y'all land," Dirty said as I helped Kami into the front seat.

"Say less." I gave him a brotherly hug and climbed into the truck. Backing out of the driveway, we headed toward the airport.

Traffic was light, so it didn't take us any time to get there.

"Bae, you got us a private jet!" Kamille yelped in excitement as we pulled into Rectrix Aerodrome Center at SRQ Airport. Parking the truck, I popped the trunk and hopped out. The Bellevue's had arranged for us to fly in on a private jet and had taken care of all the resort expenses. Kamille didn't know that this was a business/romantic getaway. All she knew was we were flying out to Colorado for Christmas. Hopefully, she wouldn't spaz out on me once she found out the truth.

"Mr. and Mrs. Howard, right this way. Welcome to RAC. We'll take care of your luggage for you," a guy with a name tag that said Frank greeted us.

Nodding my head, we followed him as he escorted us to the jet.

"Damn, slow down, bae." Slay laughed as I downed my third shot of Tequila. This was my first time flying, and I was scared as hell. Although I was excited, my nerves had started to kick in. The shots I'd taken before we left the house did little to nothing to ease my mind.

"I'm scared, Slay," I admitted.

"Everything is going to be fine. Just try to relax."

Shit, that was easy for him to say. Flying for him was normal. My ass had never been off the ground before.

"Good afternoon, passengers. This is your captain speaking. First, I'd like to welcome everyone on Aerodrome private jet 380 from Florida to Colorado. At this time, I would like to ask all passengers to put on their seatbelt and get ready for takeoff."

As the captain gave his speech, I put on my seatbelt, grabbed hold of Slay's hand, and squeezed it. I sent a silent prayer up to God to get us to Colorado in one piece as the jet began to take off.

"Ladies and gentlemen, the captain has turned off the 'fasten seat belt' sign, and you may now move around the cabin."

Thank God! I breathed a sigh of relief as I removed my seatbelt. Looking around, I took this time to admire the interior of the jet. The inside of the plane looked like a mini apartment. There were plush leather couches, a flat screen TV, a minibar, and a small kitchenette. Slay really went all out for this trip, and I was extremely impressed. Talk about classy.

"You okay?" Slay asked, rubbing my leg.

"So far." I nervously laughed as I signaled for the stewardess to bring me another drink.

"Really, babe," Slay chuckled. "C'mon, I got something that will relax you."

Grabbing my hand, he pulled me from my seat, and I follow him toward the restroom. Once inside, he locked the door behind us and began to unbuckle his pants.

"Tremell!" I hissed as I watch his pants hit the floor and his dick pop out. "What are you doing?"

"I'm about to give you something to calm you down," he said with the lick of his lips.

"Slay, we can't fuck in here."

"Why not?" He asked as he stroked himself. Just the sight of his dick made my mouth water and my pussy throb. With one thick vein running down the length of it, it was so beautiful. His smooth caramel mushroom head was just begging for me to lick it.

"What if someone hears us?"

"Shit, let 'em. Besides, this is a private jet. Ain't nobody on here but me, you, and the staff. Now, bend that ass over," Slay demanded, turning me around.

Hiking my dress up, I pulled my thong to the side and slightly opened my legs.

"Damn, she's already wet for daddy," Slay moaned as he rubbed his dick against my opening. Slowly he pushed inside of me, causing a deep moan to escape my mouth.

"Shit!" I groaned as he filled me up. No matter how many times we've had sex, I still wasn't able to take all of Slay's dick. As I adjusted to his size, he began to slowly stroke me.

"Put your leg up on the sink," he instructed, and I complied.

"Oh, my god! Slay!" I cried as he grabbed a handful of my hair, pulled my head back, and pounded into me.

"Shh! They can hear you!"

At this point, I couldn't care less who heard me. Slay was repeatedly hitting my g-spot, and I couldn't help up moan in pleasure.

"I'm about to cum, baby!" I groaned as my pussy tightened around his dick. After a few more strokes, we were cumming together.

"Fuck!" Slay roared as he released inside of me.

This was just the release I needed to get me to relax. A good nut always did it for me. After catching our breath, we cleaned ourselves up and fixed our clothes. Making sure my hair was in place, we headed back to our seats.

"Here's your drink, Mrs. Howard," the stewardess blushed while handing me my drink. I could tell she heard us having sex from the way she was looking at us. Grabbing my drink, I thanked her and enjoyed the rest of the ride.

⬤ ⬤ ⬤

"Oh my god! This is beautiful!" I gushed as we pulled up to Grand Colorado on Peak 8 Resort. This place was magnificent. If I wasn't in the Christmas spirit before, I definitely was now. The resort was decorated with Christmas lights and had all the trimmings. This was my first-time seeing snow, so I was like a kid in the candy store.

When the car stopped, the bellman opened the door for me and helped me out. I was glad I bought a new coat for this trip because it was freezing. It had to be at least twenty degrees.

"Shit, it's cold!" Slay complained, rubbing his hands together and blowing on them.

"Mr. and Mrs. Howard, right this way," the bellhop said as two other guys loaded our luggage onto a cart.

Grabbing Slay's hand, I couldn't stop myself from smiling as we walked into the resort. This was just the type of vacation I needed. Looking around the lobby, I was happy to see everything was nice, clean, and decked out in Christmas décor.

"Welcome to Grand Colorado," the clerk behind the desk greeted us with a smile.

"Tremell Howard checking in."

"Yes, Mr. Howard, your room is ready," she said as she handed Slay the room key. "Here is your itinerary for your stay from The Bellevue's. Enjoy your stay and happy holidays."

"Thanks."

"Just take the elevators up to the third floor. Once you get off, make a left, and your room will be the fourth door on the right."

Heading to the elevators, I saw a few more couples checking in. It was nice to see other couples taking advantage of such a beautiful place. Following the clerk's directions, we made it to our room and headed inside. I was happy to see that our bags were already there.

"Would you look at this place!" I gasped, looking around the room. The pictures I saw didn't do this place justice. This place was set up like an apartment. Complete with a kitchen, living room with a beautiful fireplace, a full couch, and the cutest Christmas tree. The huge bay window showed a breathtaking view of the mountains. Going into the master bedroom, there was a huge California king bed that looked so comfortable. I was going to convince Slay to get us one once we made it back home.

"So what you think?" Slay quizzed, hugging me from behind.

"Tremell, thank you so much for this trip," I said as I kissed his lips.

"Anything for my beautiful wife," he says as he hugs me tighter. Watching the snow fall was magical. I wish I could stay in this moment forever.

"I'mma start unpacking, and then we can check out the rest of the resort."

"Cool, but before we do that, we have to meet up with someone."

"Who?" I asked with a raised eyebrow.

"Just a few new acquaintances. It shouldn't take that long."

Shrugging my shoulders, I begin unpacking our bags. Once I was done, I decided to shower to wash the day off of me, not to mention I still smelled like sex. When I entered the master bathroom, my jaw dropped. Being an interior decorator, I've seen and designed some immaculate bathrooms, but this was just over the top. The ceilings were vaulted, there was his & her sinks, a huge garden tub, and a separate walk-in shower. I wanted to take advantage of the tub, but I opted to take a shower instead.

🞑 🞑 🞑

Twenty minutes later, I emerged from the bathroom feeling like new money. The water pressure in the shower was just right.

"About time," Slay joked, looking at his Rolex. I noticed that he'd changed clothes as well.

"Shut up." I laughed as I dropped my towel and began to lotion my body. I caught Slay staring at me, so I made sure to be extra when it came to applying the lotion to my thighs.

"Don't start no shit, Kami. I told you we got somewhere to be in about thirty minutes."

"Okay, dang." I pretended to pout while getting dressed. Ten minutes later, I was dressed in a beige Gucci sweater, with a pair of beige leather pants, nude and white high heeled fur boots with a coat and hat to match.

"Damn, girl, you looking good," Slay commented, licking his lips and rubbing his chin.

"I know." I smirked as I walked past him.

"Alright, Kami, don't get one of these niggas fucked up," he threatened as we walked out the door.

Looking over the itinerary for the week, I noticed a meeting being held tonight at eight p.m. Kamille wanted to check out the resort, but first, I had to handle this business. While she was in the shower, I texted Darnael to let him know that we had arrived, and I would see him at the meeting shortly.

Once Kamille finally got out of the shower, I waited for her to get dressed, then we headed downstairs to the boardroom. When we got to the boardroom, I noticed there were a few more cats there with their women as well. I thought it was just going to be me, Kami, Darnael, and his wife, Blair. This was sure to be interesting.

At exactly eight p.m., the doors opened, and we all entered the room. After greeting and shaking hands with Darnael and his wife, I found my and Kamille's seats close to the exit. I wasn't familiar with any of these niggas in this room, so I wanted to make sure I had eyes on everybody in case some shit popped off. I was strapped, and I made sure that Kamille was as well.

After everyone took their seats, the servers came around

to take our food and drink orders. I wasn't going to get too faded until after this meeting, so I went light and just ordered a shot of D'ussé. Once everyone placed their orders, and the servers left the room, Darnael stood and began to speak.

"I know many of you aren't aware of why you were hand-picked by us to be here during this holiday season. For those who don't know, my wife Blair was given sole reign over the Jimenez Cartel and passed that along to me. I could bore you all with those details, but it ain't necessary. The reason that you are all here is that you hold a particular set of skills that would be beneficial to bringing in more money than any of us could ever dream about. But enough of the introduction. Let's get down to fuckin' business."

I glanced over at Kamille, who had a blank expression on her face. I know this whole cartel thing was a shock to her. To be honest, it was a shock to me too. I've dealt with many different types of dudes from mob bosses, kingpins, and cartel leaders. But never once have I joined one. My brother and I have always run our business solo. I knew before I made a decision, I was going to have to run everything by Dirty.

While I was processing everything, one of the girls jumped up and started spazzing. I guess none of us told our women the real reason we were all on this trip.

From what I gathered, the spazzing woman's name was Aria, and her dude name was Nassir. Apparently, he used to be in the game but was taking a step back to let his homeboy handle things, and his girl wasn't too happy about him trying to come back. Then there was Eze Sadiq. He used to run an underground female fighting ring. He'd gone legit and now owned several boxing gyms in Nashville.

Last but not least, there were Erick and Armany. Armany seemed to be the one in charge because she had her own company that transported work overseas. Everyone here was going to play a major role in this new business venture.

"I'm not going to bore y'all anymore tonight, so let's use this time to toast to new beginnings," Darnael said as the servers walked in the room and began passing out champagne flutes. Together, all of us raised our glasses and toasted to the future.

"Welcome to Hustla's Holiday in Colorado. On behalf of my wife and me, we would like to welcome everyone to the Jimenez Cartel. I know decisions haven't been set in stone, but hopefully, once this is all over, we will be partners for a long time."

"So that's what this entire trip was about, Tremell? A chance for you to join some damn drug cartel!" I screamed.

To say I was pissed was an understatement. I was fucking livid. I was able to keep my composure during the entire meeting, but as soon as we got back to the room, I let his ass have it. I can't believe this shit. Here I thought we came up here to enjoy a nice Christmas getaway for just the two of us, but it all turned out to be a business trip.

"Kami, calm down."

"Don't tell me to calm down, Slay! Why didn't you tell me this before we left Florida? You had me thinking this week was all about us when it really was all about you."

"It is about us!"

"I can't fucking tell!"

Kicking my shoes off, I snatched off my coat and threw it on the couch. Stomping to the bedroom, I made sure to slam the door hard as fuck. Plopping down on the bed, I grabbed the room phone and called Yandy.

"Hello."

"Hey, girl." I sighed heavily.

"Ew! Why you sound like that?"

"Girl, you won't believe the shit Slay just pulled."

I ran down the entire meeting to her as she listened intensely.

"Kami, you know, as your best friend, I'm going to keep it real with you. I think you're overreacting."

"What?" I shouted, taking the phone away from my ear and looking at it.

"I mean, yes, he was wrong for not telling you, but that's no reason to be mad at the man the entire trip. Slay is a very smart dude. I'm sure he won't get into anything that would bring harm to you, him, or Dirty. All he's trying to do is make a little extra money and expand his business."

"It's not the fact that he's trying to expand his business. It's the fact that he lied to me, Yandy. If he would've told me he would handle business on this trip, I would've been fine with that. You know I would never get in the way of him making money."

"I feel you, but don't let it ruin your trip. You are at a beautiful resort in the mountains. Slay made sure that while he handled business, he was able to grant you your childhood wish. It's the holidays, Kami. Stop being so damn grumpy, bitch!" Yandy laughed.

Leave it to Yandy to set me straight. We talked for a little while longer before saying our goodbyes. Although I was still mad at Slay, I felt like I should apologize for yelling at him. Getting up from the bed, I left the room in search of him. I found him standing out on the balcony, smoking a blunt. Walking up behind him, I wrapped my arms around his waist and laid my head on his back.

"I'm sorry," I mumbled.

"I love you, Kami," he said, turning around and kissing me on the forehead. "Understand that I would never do anything to jeopardize the safety of my family. This is a great business move, and I wouldn't even consider it if I thought I would bring bullshit to our front door."

"I know that baby, and I trust you. This whole thing just caught me off guard. I thought this week was going to just be about us."

"It is about us. I've handled my business, and now I can focus on us. We can do whatever you want to do."

"You promise?"

"I have ever lied to you?"

Kissing his lips, I apologize again before we decided to order room service and call it a night. We've had a long day, and I had to admit I was tired. Since he said the rest of the trip was about us, I was going to make him stand on that.

"What the fuck?" I yelled, quickly jumping out of bed.

Looking around the room, I saw Kamille standing by the door laughing like shit was funny. This crazy ass woman had just thrown snow on me while I was asleep. That shit was cold as hell on my bare back.

"Let's hit the slopes!"

"Hit what?"

"The slopes, babe. I want to go skiing."

"Kamille, what the hell do you know about skiing? You ain't ever did that shit before," I argued as I headed to the bathroom to take a leak.

"I know Slay, but I want to try," she whined, leaning against the door frame.

Flushing the toilet, I washed my hands, brushed my teeth, and washed my face. Kamille was out of her damn mind talking about going skiing.

"Kami, we are from Florida, okay. Real niggas don't ski. That's that white boy shit."

"Please, bae," she pouted, coming over to the sink and rubbing her hands against my dick.

Kamille thought she was slick, but I wasn't falling for that shit. She could rub on my dick all she wanted, but I was a true Floridan, and the only thing I knew how to do was swim. If she thought she would get me on the top of a mountain, she could forget it.

◆ ◆ ◆

I can't believe I let Kamille talk me into this shit. Here I was, freezing my ass off in zero-degree weather, with skis strapped to my feet. I don't know why I listened to her ass when she said this would be easy. I'd fallen three times, and I couldn't feel my damn ears. My ass was numb, and I think I twisted my ankle.

"Isn't this fun?" Kamille squealed in delight as she came toward me.

"Man, hell naw! I'm freezing my ass off out here, Kami. Plus, I've busted my ass three times since we've been here. Let's go back to the room so I can warm up."

"Slay, we did not come here to sit in the room all weekend. Remember, you said this trip was all about us, and it was whatever I wanted."

I could kick my own ass for saying that shit.

"Bae—"

"I tell you what," she says, cutting me off. "Let's do one more thing, and then we can head back to the room."

I looked at her sideways because, at this moment, I didn't trust her ass. She was liable to ask me to bungee jump or some shit, and I wasn't with it.

"What is it, Kamille? I'm telling you right now, if it's some bullshit, I'm leaving you right out here."

"It's going to be fun. I promise." She laughed, kissing me on the lips.

Taking my skis off, I follow her back to the rental booth to return them. After walking a few feet, we ended up at another rental booth with tubes.

"What's this?" I asked.

"We're going to go tubing down the mountain."

"What?"

Never in my life had I heard of people tubing down the side of a mountain. At this point, I was convinced Kamille was trying to kill me.

"It's simple. All we do is sit down in the tube, and they push us down the mountain. It's like the rides at Adventure Island."

The rides at Adventure Island weren't bad because you were sliding down a slide. This shit was different. This was a damn mountain! There were trees and the risk of flying off the side of this muthafucka.

"How about I stay here and watch you?" I suggested.

Placing her hands on her hips, Kami gave me the death stare. Deciding I'd rather take my chances flying off the side of the mountain than playing with her, I got my ass in the tube.

◻ ◻ ◻

Aside from my ass being numb, I had to admit it wasn't as bad as I thought it would be. After returning the tube, we headed back to the room to change clothes and warm up. Checking my phone, I saw that Dirty had called twice while we were out, so I decided to give him a call back.

"Bro! What's good nigga?" he answered.

"Enjoying life, man. What's up with you?"

"Shit the same. Business is business, so ain't no complaints there. I was calling to let you know I thought about what you said, and I'm down."

Yes! That was exactly the type of news I needed to hear. Now that Dirty was on board, we could move forward with doing business with Darnael and Blair. I really couldn't make this move without him, so I was glad he agreed.

"That's what's up, bro. I promise you this a good move."

"If I don't trust nobody else, I trust you."

We talked for a little while longer before hanging up. I planned on meeting up with the fellas the following day, so I would let Darnael know that everything was straight on my end.

Stepping out of the shower, I wrapped the plush white towel around my body and exited the bathroom. Grabbing my body butter from Layah's Boutique, I sat down on the bed and began to moisturize my skin.

"Damn, you smell good," Slay complimented, walking into the room. Smiling up at him, I continued getting ready.

"Come here," Slay groaned, pulling me up by my waist.

"Slay, stop!" I giggled as he tried to remove my towel. "You're going to make me late."

Blair had arranged a spa day for all us ladies, and I couldn't wait to get a massage. At first, I wasn't going to go, but Slay convinced me to. I guess since he was thinking about doing business with the other men, he wanted me to get aquatinted with their wives. From the first meeting we had, it seemed like the ladies were okay. I wasn't too friendly when it came to other females, but for my husband, I would try.

"Just give me a little before you go. You know we ain't gone see each other until tonight."

While I was getting pampered at the spa, Slay was going to be hanging out with the fellas.

"Now you know damn well once we start, we gone be fucking for a while. Besides, I gave you some last night."

"Well, let me at least taste you, shit."

Say less! I thought to myself as I quickly dropped my towel and laid back on the bed. Never would I turn down head from my husband.

"Look at you, game for that shit." He chuckled.

Grabbing my ankles, he pulled me to the edge of the bed. Getting on his knees, he placed my legs on my shoulders and just stared at my pussy for a minute. With two fingers, he spread my pussy lips apart. When his warm tongue touched my clit, I screamed in ecstasy. The way he sucked and licked on my pearl had me gripping the sheets and speaking in tongues.

"Ahh!" I moaned and arched my back. This shit had to be illegal what he was doing to me.

"Stop running from me!" Slay growled, gripping my thighs tighter. Now I couldn't run if I wanted to. I'd been lost count of how many times I came. He was eating me like I was his last meal, and I had to say that I damn sure was enjoying it.

"Tremell!" I screamed as my stomach muscles tightened, and my legs shook. Gripping the back of his head, I pushed his face further into my pussy as I came on his tongue.

"Damn girl, you wet up the whole bed." Slay laughed with my pussy juices glistening on his beard. I watched as he wiped his face off.

"Give me some dick," I demanded, reaching for his dick.

"Naw," he said, stepping back. "I don't want to make you late."

"Slay, stop playing with me!" I practically screamed. I was so horny my pelvis was aching.

"I'll see you later on tonight, baby. The guys are waiting on me. Love you, wife," he threw over his shoulder on his way out the door.

"Slay!" Ugh! I can't believe he left before giving me some dick. He was dead ass wrong, but it's okay because I would get his ass back.

Glancing over at the clock on the wall, I realized I only had ten minutes to make it to the spa. Sprinting back toward the bathroom, I quickly wiped myself off and got dressed. With five minutes to spare, I ran from the room in search of the spa.

"Welcome to Infinity Spa," the hostess greeted me with a smile.

"Hi! I'm Kamille Howard, and I'm a guest of Mrs. Bellevue."

"Oh, yes. Mrs. Bellevue and her other guest are inside. Right, this way."

I follow her to the locker room, where she hands me a brand new white plush rode with the resort's name on it and a pair of white plush slippers. Thanking her, I quickly changed my clothes and headed to join the other ladies.

"Hello, ladies!" I smiled as I took a seat in one of the comfortable chairs.

"Hey!" they all said in unison.

Grabbing a glass of champagne from the server, I took a sip and marveled at the taste. I made a mental note to get the name of this champagne before we left. A few minutes later, another woman walked in. She greeted us, and we all begin to talk and get to know each other. As we were chatting, SunJai revealed to us that she was pregnant with her second child. I could tell she was happy about it, but there was something else bothering her.

"Trouble in paradise?" I asked, leaning forward in my seat

to get a little more comfortable.

As she began to talk, I soaked it all in. It was amazing the background some of these women had. You had SunJai who was kidnapped and sold to her now boyfriend Eze and forced into an underground fighting ring. Blair who used to run a cartel but passed it to her husband, Darnael. Armany who was married to Erick and trafficked drug across seas. Then there was Aria. She was the one popping off at the first meet and greet because her husband Nassir was thinking about jumping back into the game. These were some badass women, and I respected them all. I mean, just looking at them, you could never tell the life they lived.

After drinking a few more glasses of champagne and talking a little more, we all went to another room to get our massages. Taking my robe off, I laid flat on the warm massage table. As the woman worked my muscles, I drifted off to sleep.

⬧ ⬧ ⬧

"Come on, Kami! Our reservations are for eight o'clock!" Slay yelled through the bathroom door. His ass was always rushing me to go somewhere. Taking a final look at myself in the mirror, I sprayed on my YSL Black Opium perfume and exited the bathroom.

"About time."

"Shut up." I laughed playfully hitting him with my clutch bag.

We were on our way to dinner at the resort hotel. They had a five-star restaurant that served some of the best food from what I read online.

"Reservation for Howard," Slay announced when we got to the restaurant. Following the host to our table, I took in my surroundings. The restaurant was quite busy. The sound of cheerful laughter and light background music created a pleasant ambiance.

"Thank you," I said as the host pulled out my chair. A few minutes later, our waitress came over to introduce herself and take our drink orders.

"Are you enjoying yourself?" Slay asked.

"This place is so beautiful. Thank you again for this trip."

We talked about our day and Slay told me that he was joining the cartel. At first, I was a little nervous about him joining, but after talking with Blair and the other women, I was a little more comfortable. After our drinks arrived, we placed our food order. I was really enjoying my husband's company until...

"Well, look who it is."

The hair stood up on the back of my neck. I knew that voice anywhere. Slowly turning around, my blood began to boil.

"Lacey! What the fuck are you doing here?"

That's right bitches I'm back. If Slay thought he was going to get away from me, he had another thing coming. The look on both he and Kamille's face when I popped up on their ass was priceless.

"Lacey! What the fuck are you doing here?" Slay yelled.

If looks could kill, I would be one dead bitch from the way Kamille was glaring at me. I couldn't care less about how that bitch was feeling. She stole my man, and I was going to make it my business to fuck up their little marriage.

"Well, I thought it would be nice to go on a little Christmas vacation. Funny running into you here." I smiled a wicked smile.

Truth is, I was snooping around on Slay's Yahoo account and saw a confirmation e-mail for a flight to Colorado. When Slay and I were dating, I used to always book us trips, so I had access to his account. I guess he never felt the need to change the password, which worked out in my favor. My plan was to pop up on his ass and ruin their Christmas vacation. What pissed me off the most was the fact that the nigga never took me to the mountains. He got with this bitch and started showing out.

"Lacey, get the fuck away from our table before I show out in this bitch," Slay demanded, grabbing me by my arm and pushing me away.

"Don't put your fucking hands on me!" I screamed, snatching away from him and causing a scene.

"Is everything okay?" the restaurant manager asked, rushing over to us.

"No! This nigga just put his fucking hands on me!"

"My wife and I were enjoying our dinner when this bit… woman came up bothering us."

"Ma'am, I'm going to have to ask you to leave," the manager had the nerve to tell me. How dare he try to kick me out when I was a paying guest?

"I'm a guest here!" I argued as I watched resort security quickly approach.

"Ma'am, please. You're causing a scene, and it's disturbing our other guests. Now, if you don't leave, I'll be forced to have security escort you out."

Looking around the restaurant, I saw that all eyes were on us. Perfect. This is just what I wanted. Looking over at Kamille, she looked as if she wanted to cry, which made my soul smile. Deciding that I'd already succeeded in ruining their dinner, I blew Slay a kiss and left the restaurant. They just didn't know just how bad I was going to fuck their little vacation up.

☐ ☐ ☐

"Girl, that bitch looked like she wanted to cry!" I laughed into the phone as I talked to my homegirl Vanessa on the phone. It brought me joy to know that I had ruined Slay's little dinner date with his so-called wife. That bitch could roll over and die for all I cared.

"Slay is gone beat yo' ass, bitch. I still can't believe you did that shit," Vanessa voiced.

I could just picture Vanessa shaking her head. When I first told her about my plans to fly to Colorado and fuck up Slay's Christmas, she tried to talk me out of it. She felt as if I was crazy for flying halfway across the country for a man who was happily married. Vanessa felt as if I should just leave Slay alone and move on with my life, but I couldn't do that.

I felt like I was cheated out of our relationship when he met that bitch Kamille. Ever since we broke up, my life has been in shambles. I lived with my sister, which I hated, and I couldn't find a decent job because I had no real skills. Because I couldn't find a decent job, I lost my car and was now catching Uber's everywhere. When I was with Slay, I didn't have to worry about anything. He always made sure my pockets were laced, I stayed in the newest fashion, and I had the flyest ride. With Slay, I was the baddest bitch. Without Slay, I was just another broke bitch from Royal Village. Don't get me wrong. I loved Slay, but I loved his money more.

"Well, believe it bitch because I'm here. I spend my last to come on this trip, and I'm determined to get my man back."

"Lacey, Slay doesn't want you. If he wanted you, he would've never left you for Kamille. I hate to say it, but friend, you're being stupid."

Oh no the fuck she didn't just call me stupid! This bitch had her nerve. As much as I've seen her be dumb for a nigga, she had the nerve to come at me sideways. Deciding that this conversation was over, I hung up on her without even saying goodbye. Plugging my phone into the charger, I headed to the bathroom to soak in the tub. Tomorrow was another day, and I planned on being fully rested so I could continue to be a pain in Slay's and Kamille's ass.

"What the fuck is she doing here, Slay?" I screamed as soon as we got back to the room.

The last thing I expected was to see Slay's ex-girlfriend Lacey. Lacey has been a pain in both of our asses since we met. It's like the bitch had a hard time letting go. Slay and I have been married for two years, and this bitch was still chasing him. I didn't come all the way to Colorado to catch a case, but I promise if this bitch said one thing to me, I was going to kill her and bury her in the snow.

"I don't know, Kami. The crazy bitch must've followed us here," Slay explained, trying to touch me, but I pulled away from him.

"How the fuck did she know where we were?"

"Kamille, you're asking me all these questions as if I have the answer to them. I'm just as shocked as you are."

"Termell, I swear to God—"

"Look, don't worry about it, baby. I'll handle it."

"I bet you will nigga. How the fuck are you going to tell me not to worry when that bitch has been a problem since I met yo' ass!"

"Why the fuck are you yelling at me like I asked the bitch to come here?"

No, he did not just yell at me. Smacking my teeth, I pushed past him and went to the bathroom. Once inside, I sat down on the toilet and cried. I was crying because I was upset. I knew Slay had nothing to do with Lacey showing up here, but I was still pissed. Everything was going great until that bitch popped up. Seeing her face just ruined my entire trip.

After crying for about twenty minutes, I decided I needed to clear my head. Being in this room was making me sick. When I came out of the bathroom, Slay was sitting on the couch with his eyes closed. I could see the stress all over his face, but I was in my feelings too, so I wasn't going to comfort him.

"I'm going to get some fresh air," I mumbled as I grabbed my coat and put on my boots. He didn't even flinch as I left the room.

⬬ ⬬ ⬬

"Bitch I know you lying!" Yandy screamed into the phone.

"I wish I were, girl. This bitch followed us all the way to Colorado with this bullshit. At this point, the entire trip is ruined. I just want to come home," I sobbed into the phone while wiping away my tears. I hated that I let that bitch get me like this. I just wanted that bitch to disappear. Here I was in Colorado at the most beautiful resort with my husband, and I was crying. This was not how I envision my Christmas vacation going.

"Do you need me to catch a flight to come beat her ass?"

"No." I laughed. Yandy's ass was always ready to fuck some shit up.

"Are you sure because it's nothing."

"No. That wouldn't solve anything, plus I don't want you to

get in any trouble behind Lacey's stupid ass. I got it covered."

As I continued to talk to Yandy, an idea popped into my head. I knew just what I needed to do to get rid of Lacey's ass once and for all.

"Fuck!" I yelled as Kamille walked out the door. This shit could not be happening right now.

To say seeing Lacey was a surprise would be an understatement. Never in a million years did I expect to see my crazy ass ex here. Since Kamille and I have been together, Lacey has tried everything in her power to come between us. She and Kamille have fought. Lacey's smashed out my truck windows, played on both of our phones, and still talks all kinds of shit about us on social media. The shit was annoying as fuck, but I never let it get to me. I knew Lacey was just bitter.

Kamille, on the other hand, couldn't stand the ground Lacey walked on. I hated that my wife had to go through this shit, but I couldn't control Lacey's ass. I mean, I could've paid somebody to off her ass, but I wasn't that type of dude when it came to women.

What pissed me off the most was the fact that Kamille was blaming me for this shit. She acts as if I invited Lacey's stupid ass here. Shit, I was just as mad as she was. No way in hell I would play those types of games, especially considering just how important this week was. I didn't want Darnael and the rest of the fellas to feel as if I was bringing drama to the crew. I had too much shit riding on this trip. Against my better judgment, I decided to go holla at this bitch Lacey before shit really hit the fan. I'd have to deal with my wife later. I already knew when she came back, she would give a nigga the silent treatment, so I was prepared for that.

▢ ▢ ▢

Getting Lacey's room number wasn't as hard as I thought it was going to be. I thought for sure I would have to bribe the front desk clerk with a few dollars, but she happily gave it to me. As I stood outside of Lacey's room, I braced myself for the bullshit. God knows I didn't want to lay hands on her, but if she took me there, her ass was as good as whooped. Knocking on the door, I waited for her to answer.

"I knew you would come looking for me." Lacey smiled as soon as she opened the door. Quickly rushing into her room, I forcefully pushed her against the wall.

"What the fuck are you doing here, Lacey?" I growled through gritted teeth. Never in my life did I want to hit a woman as bad as I wanted to smack her ass right now.

"I told you. I just so happen—"

"Bullshit!" I yelled, grabbing her around the neck.

"Get the fuck off of me, Tremell!" she screamed, trying to buck against me, but I was too strong. At this point, I was willing to choke the shit out of this bitch if she lied again. No way in hell was this a coincidence.

"Stop fucking lying, bitch! Yo stupid ass followed us here."

"So what if I did! Let me go!" she yelled, and I pushed her away from me. Stupid ass bitch!

"How the fuck did you even know we were here?"

"I logged into your e-mail account and saw the confirmation e-mail. I guess somebody forgot to change his passwords once we broke up." She smirked.

Hearing that, I made a mental note to change everything once I got back to the room, from bank accounts to the alarm system at the house. Ain't no telling what else this sneaky ass bitch knew.

"Stay the fuck away from me before I hurt you, Lacey," I warned her. "This stalking me shit has got to stop. There will never be an us again, and the sooner you get that through your head, the better off you will be. I'm a married fucking man, and I take my marriage seriously."

I could tell I hurt her feelings when I said that, but I couldn't care less. Lacey could go to hell for all I cared. Her popping up here was a clear sign that I made the right decision to stop fucking with her ass. She was too fucking childish.

"Fuck you, Slay! You cheated on me with that hoe and think I'm just supposed to forget about it."

"Our relationship was over before I even met Kamille, and you know it."

I can't believe she was still on this bullshit. I told her ass a long time ago to move the fuck on. If Lacey were the last bitch on earth, I would jack my dick before I ever fucked her again.

"So you can bring this bitch on expensive trips and not me!"

"What the fuck are you talking about? I don't fuck with you, and Kamille is my wife, so watch your fucking mouth."

"I just don't understand, Slay. We were together for years, and not once did you ask me to marry you. You met this bitch for two seconds and turned around and married her. What does she have that I don't!"

At this point, Lacey's face was a snotty mess, and I wasn't moved. She could cry a fucking river as far as I was concerned.

"You want to know why shit wasn't going to work between

us, Lacey? Because I found out that you cheated on me. Not only did you cheat, but you got pregnant. You didn't know whether the baby was mine or that nigga's, so you snuck and had an abortion and told me you had a miscarriage."

I could tell from the look on her face she was shocked that I knew that. I wasn't here to play games with her tired ass. I was here to let her know to stay the fuck away from my wife and me for the last time.

"Slay, I can explain."

"There's no need just stay the fuck away from my wife and me before I hurt you. The first thing in the morning, I want you to book a flight and go the fuck home."

"Slay—"

"If I see yo ass again, it won't be nice, and you know I don't make empty threats."

With that, I left her room, making sure to slam the door hard as fuck. I prayed for her sake that she gets the fuck out of dodge because I won't be responsible for the way I act if I saw her ass again.

Christmas Eve

Nervously I paced the hallway, trying to get my thoughts together. Never in my life have I done something like this, but I felt it was necessary. This bitch Lacey had been a pain in my ass since day one, and I was sick of her. Slay said he had everything under control, but I needed to take matters into my own hands. Here it was Christmas eve, and I was planning on taking a bitch out instead of enjoying hot chocolate in front of the fireplace wrapped in my husband's arms.

Last night was the first night since we've been together that we didn't sleep in the same bed. When I came back from my walk, he wasn't in the room. I figured he'd gone down to the bar to have a few drinks to blow off some steam. When he came back to the room, he posted up on the couch watching TV. That's where he fell asleep. I cried all night because my feelings were hurt. If I had any doubt in my mind that Lacey had to go, it all disappeared when my husband and I slept apart. This bitch was drawing a wedge between us, and I couldn't have that.

Blowing out a deep breath, I raised my hand and knocked on the door. I wasn't even sure if she was in the room, but I had to see. About a minute later, I heard the locks being turned, and the door swung open.

"Kamille." Blair smiled at me.

"Hey Blair, I hope I'm not interrupting you guys."

"Naw, girl you good. What's up?"

"Well," I said nervously. I didn't know how to just ask her for help. "I have this situation that I need your help with. Is it okay if we talk in private?"

"Yeah, just let me grab my shoes. Hold on."

While Blair went to grab her shoes, I started to have second thoughts. I mean, could I really go through with this shit?

"Okay, talk to me, girl. What's going on?"

"Okay. Long story short, Slay's ex is here starting shit. Apparently, she followed us here on some stalker shit. Slay said he handled it, but I know once we make it back home, that bitch is still going to be on bullshit."

"You know what? Don't even worry about it. I got just the thing for her ass."

I watched as she got up and went back into her room. A short second later, she come back out.

"You look like you're about to throw up. Please don't throw up in front of my door."

She was right. My hands were sweaty, and my stomach was churning. I'm sure all the color had drained from my face.

"Girl, I've never done shit like this."

Blair looked at me with shock written all over her face. I guess she thought since being with Slay, I was into the life like her and the other ladies, but I wasn't. I owned a designing company, for Christ's sake! Taking a few deep breathes, I counted to ten to calm down.

Reaching into her coat pocket, Blair pulled out a bottle of pills. Showing them to me, she gave me the rundown on just what to do with them.

"And this stays between us, okay? If my husband finds out, bitch I'm dead."

"Right."

Thanking her, I gave her a hug and headed back to my room. That bitch Lacey was going to learn today.

󠀀 󠀀 󠀀

"Bae," Slays spoke, shaking me awake.

"Um," I mumbled, pulling the covers over my head. I was tired as hell and didn't want to be bothered.

"Wake up, Kami. I have to tell you something."

Sighing, I slowly take the covers off my head. This had better be good.

"What's going on, baby?"

"They found Lacey dead in her room."

"What?" I yelled quickly, sitting up.

"Yeah. I just got a phone call from Blair telling me they found a body, and it was Lacey's."

"Well, do they know what happened?"

"Naw, there was no blood or anything. Blair said it looks like she just died in her sleep."

"Damn," I whispered, trying to keep a smile from forming on my face.

I knew exactly how that bitch died. Those pills Blair showed me were Fentanyl. I crushed the entire bottle up and put it in a bottle of champagne, and had it sent to her room along with some flowers. As delusional as the bitch was, I knew she would be happy to receive it, thinking it was from Slay.

"This shit crazy," Slay said as he sat down on the bed.

"How are you feeling?" I asked as if I gave a fuck. I was glad the bitch was dead. I made a mental note to send Blair something nice for looking out for me.

"I mean, it is what it is, shit. I ain't gone sit up and say I don't feel a little bad for her family, but I ain't gone shed a tear either. Lacey was a pain in my ass, and now we don't have to worry about her anymore." He shrugged.

Climbing behind him, I wrapped my arms around him and kissed his neck. He smelled like he'd just gotten out of the shower. For some reason, hearing that Lacey was dead turned me on in the worst way. As I continued to kiss his neck and rub on his chest, I could see his dick rise in his gym shorts. He got up and turned around to face me. His dick was staring me right in the face, and I couldn't wait to taste him.

Pulling my shirt off over my head, I tied my hair up into a messy bun. Reaching for his gym shorts, I pulled them down, and his dick sprung out like a Jack-in-the-box. Grabbing it at the base, I wet my mouth and slowly licked the head.

"Um," Slay moaned.

Inch by inch, I began to take him into my mouth. I could feel the head of his dick hit the back of my throat, and that made my mouth wetter.

"Fuck, Kami!" Slay yelled as I being to hum on his dick. I learned that little trick from a book I read.

He grabbed a fistful of my hair and began to fuck my mouth. I had spit spilling out the side of my mouth and onto my breasts, but I didn't care. I was making up for the way I acted last night. My husband has been nothing but good to me since day one, and I wanted to show my appreciation.

"Bend that ass over!" Slay demanded, taking his dick from

my mouth. Happily, I got on all fours and arched my back just the way he liked it.

"Oh!" I yelped when he smacked me on the ass.

Spreading my ass cheeks apart, I damn there flew off the bed when he stuck his tongue in my ass. That shit felt so good. Slay was a freak and had turned my ass out. As I threw my ass back on his face, my pussy became wetter. When his tongue ticked my clit, I couldn't help the orgasm that shot through my body.

"Ahh!" I screamed as my body shook from pleasure. I collapse on the bed because my knees had gone weak.

"Toot that ass back up. I ain't done with you yet," Slay exclaimed, pulling me up by my hips. Lining his dick up to my pussy, he roughly entered me. I tried to run, but he pulled me back.

"Take this dick, don't run from it!" he growled, grabbing my hair and pulling my head back.

"Fuck me!" I screamed, not giving a damn who heard. Slay was fucking me like a savage, and I loved every minute of it.

By the time we were done fucking, my pussy was sore, and I was spent. I wanted to get up and take a shower, but I was too weak to move. Now, this is how I wanted to spend Christmas Eve.

I woke up early this morning to get a head start on my day. Today was going to be very eventful, and I wanted to make sure everything was in place. We weren't scheduled to be at the service for another three hours, so we had time. My man's Eze had something special planned for his girl SunJai, and he wanted us all in attendance.

Peeping in the room at Kamille, I smiled to myself. I knew she was tired from the dick I laid on her last night, so I would let her sleep until room service arrived. I was glad we were back on speaking terms because I couldn't stand when we were at odds. It killed me sleeping on the couch the other night and not in the bed with my wife. That bitch Lacey had tried to fuck up our vacation, but unfortunately for her, that shit didn't work.

Finding out Lacey had died was shocking, but I would be lying if I said I wasn't glad. Had she stayed her ass in Florida, maybe she would still be alive. I really don't know what happened to her, but I knew that everything happened for a reason.

Grabbing my phone, I called my family to wish everyone a

Merry Christmas. Kamille and I decided that we would exchange gifts when we got back home, but I still had something special planned for her. As I wrapped up a conversation with my mother, there was a knock at the door. Jogging to the door, I looked out the peephole before opening it.

"Here you are, Mr. Howard," the guy from room service said, pushing the cart into the room.

Thanking him, I handed him a fifty-dollar tip and sent him on his way. The aroma of the food made my stomach growl, so I quickly set the table and headed to the room to wake Kamille.

"Bae," I said, shaking her, "breakfast is here. Get up so we can eat. We got a long day ahead of us."

"Okay," she mumbled.

About fifteen minutes later she joined me at the breakfast table. Once we were done eating, we took a quick shower, got dressed, and headed downstairs to the service.

As Eze and SunJai shared their vows, I wiped a lone tear from my cheek. This reminded me of when Slay and I got married. That was one of the happiest days of my life. I was so happy for SunJai because all she wanted was to marry the love of her life, and it was finally happening. When Slay told me about Eze's plan to marry SunJai on Christmas day, I was overly excited. I knew she didn't suspect a thing, so I knew this was going to be a day she would never forget.

"That was so beautiful," I gushed as they shared a kiss. SunJai was glowing, and that rock on her finger was stunning.

Slay said there was a Christmas Gala/wedding reception in the main ballroom later on after the service. I wish he had mentioned a gala before we came because I didn't have shit to wear. Being that it was Christmas day, I doubt there were any stores open for me to go grab something real quick. I guess I was going to have to throw something together.

"Did you hear about the guest who died in her sleep?" I overheard someone say as we were leaving the service.

Glancing over at Blair, we shared a knowing look. I was glad that bitch Lacey would no longer be a problem. It felt good to know that my husband and I could live the rest of our lives without that dizzy bitch interfering in our marriage.

"I got a surprise for you back at the room," Slay revealed, causing a smile to cover my face. If his gift were anything like last night, I wasn't sure we would make it to the gala tonight.

Walking into the ballroom, I had to say that I was impressed. Blair and Darnael had this place decked out to the fullest. It reminded me of a winter wonderland. The DJ was cutting up, and I couldn't wait to get out on the dance floor. As we walked around, I spotted the other ladies and waved at them. Finding our table, we took a seat and were both handed a glass of champagne.

"You look beautiful tonight, baby," Slay complimented me.

The surprise he had for me was a red Valentino gown with a beautiful headpiece to match. He knew how I was about my appearance, and I didn't want to go to the gala half stepping.

"Thank you, baby. You are looking good too."

I smiled as I admired him in his tailored Armani suit. My man looked good enough to eat, and that is exactly what I planned on doing once we got back to the room.

As I danced in my seat and drank champagne, the doors opened, and Eze and SunJai walked in.

"Y'all, put your hands together and give it up for Eze and

SunJai Sadiq!" the DJ yelled over the music. Standing to my feet I cheered and clapped for them.

"I'll be right back, baby. I'mma go congratulate Eze," Slay informed, kissing me on the cheek.

"Congratulations, nigga!" I stated as I dappled Eze up.

"Appreciate that, man," he replied as the server came over and gave us each a bottle of champagne.

Popping the cork, I brought the bottle to my lips and took a drink. Soon after, the DJ started playing Jeezy's "Here We Go" and the real party began.

It felt good to turn up with the fellas. Now that we were all doing business together, things could only go up from here. Taking another drink from my champagne bottle, I felt on top of the world. Who knew the year was going to end like this?

I glanced over at Kamille who was on the dance floor with the other ladies throwing her ass in a circle to "Pussy Talk" by The City Girls. If we were anywhere else, I would've snatched her ass up, but since we were amongst family, I let her have her fun. After watching the women dance for a little while longer, we decided to join them.

"Alright now, keep throwing yo' ass back on me like that," I directed into Kamille's ear as I pushed my erection into her.

"What you gone do?" She smirked and made her ass clap. See, she was gone make a nigga take her in the bathroom and do her dirty.

As we grind on each other, the music suddenly stops, and Darnael grabbed the mic.

"I would like to formally welcome everyone to the Jimenez family. It's only up from here!" He lifted his glass, and we all followed suit. Just then, "Silent Night" by The Temptations started playing.

"Aye! You know this my shit!" Kamille yelled as she wrapped her arms around my neck. We swayed back and forth, whispering nasty shit in each other's ears.

For the rest of the night, we turned up and got drunk with the crew. I wish my brother were here to turn up with me, but we had time for that. This was the fucking life, and I was going to enjoy every moment.

CHAPTER 14

"Kamille, baby, hurry up. The truck will be here any minute to take us to the airport!" Slay yelled through the bathroom door.

"I'm coming, bae!" I yelled back as I put the final touches on his gift. Looking myself over in the mirror, I took a deep breath and exited the bathroom.

"Damn, what you were in there doing, taking a shit?" Slay laughed as I entered the living room.

"Ew! Shut up." I laughed playfully hitting him on the arm.

"Mr. and Mrs. Howard, your transportation has arrived," the bellhop announced from the door.

"Thank you. Let's go, woman," Slay said, heading toward the door.

"Wait! Before we go, I wanted to give you something."

"Babe, you can give me some coochie on the jet."

Here." I laughed as I handed Slay his gift. He makes me so sick.

"I thought we weren't going to exchange gifts until we got home," he stated, confused as he took the gift from my hand.

I stood back nervously as he slowly unwrapped the wrapping paper.

"Are you serious?" he asked as excitement danced around in his eyes.

"Yes!" I nodded my head as tears ran down my face.

"Hell yeah! He shouted as he scooped me up and spun me

around. Slay always wanted kids, and the positive pregnancy test that I just gave him was a new chapter in our lives together.

"Merry Christmas, baby."

"Merry Christmas, bae."

THE END

Merry Christmas
& A Happy New Year!
from Slay & Kamille

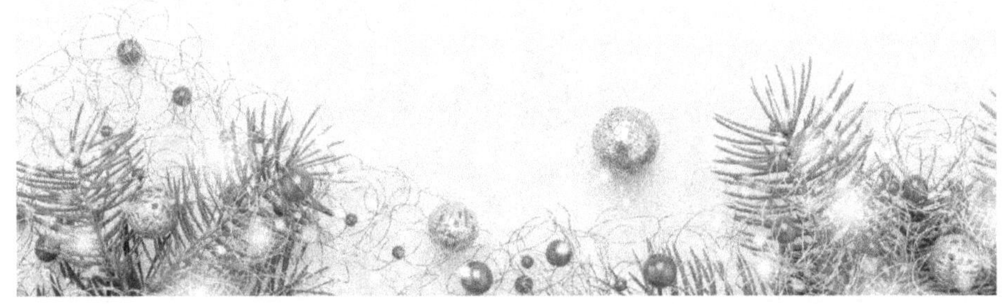

❖❖Keeping Up With Tip❖❖

Thank you for reading! Please be sure to leave a review and check out my catalog below.

When Hood Love Hurts

When Hood Love Hurts 2

Once Upon A Hood Love: A Palm Beach Fairytale (Novella)

A Single Red Rose: A Tale Of Domestic Violence (Novella)

'Tis The Season To Trap (Novella)

Enticed By A Don (Standalone)

Tarnished: Everything That Glitters (Standalone)

In My Projects: Love & War In Royal Village (Standalone)

Tears Of A Broken Heart

Tears Of A Broken Heart 2

STAY CONNECTED

Facebook: Tip Montana

Facebook Like Page: Montana's Place

Instagram: Tip_Montana

E-mail: Tipcrawford@yahoo.com

Tip Montana
The Author

Fab
FIVE